540 L

R0201666955

11/2020

W9-AYO-576

A Note to Parents and Caregivers:

Read-it! Readers are for children who are just starting on the amazing road to reading. These beautiful books support both the acquisition of reading skills and the love of books.

The PURPLE LEVEL presents basic topics and objects using high frequency words and simple language patterns.

The RED LEVEL presents familiar topics using common words and repeating sentence patterns.

The BLUE LEVEL presents new ideas using a larger vocabulary and varied sentence structure.

The YELLOW LEVEL presents more challenging ideas, a broad vocabulary, and wide variety in sentence structure.

The GREEN LEVEL presents more complex ideas, an extended vocabulary range, and expanded language structures.

The ORANGE LEVEL presents a wide range of ideas and concepts using challenging vocabulary and complex language structures.

When sharing a book with your child, read in short stretches, pausing often to talk about the pictures. Have your child turn the pages and point to the pictures and familiar words. And be sure to reread favorite stories or parts of stories.

There is no right or wrong way to share books with children. Find time to read with your child, and pass on the legacy of literacy.

Adria F. Klein, Ph.D.
Professor Emeritus
California State University
San Bernardino, California

Editor: Christianne Jones
Designer: Hilary Wacholtz
Art Director: Nathan Gassman
The illustrations in this book were created with watercolor and pencil.

Picture Window Books
A Capstone Imprint
1710 Roe Crest Drive
North Mankato, MN 56003
877-845-8392
www.capstonepub.com

Library of Congress Cataloging-in-Publication Data
Klein, Adria F. (Adria Fay), 1947-
Max goes to the farmers' market / by Adria F. Klein ; illustrated by
Mernie Gallagher-Cole.
p. cm. — (Read-it! readers. The life of Max)
ISBN 978-1-4048-5263-1 (hardcover)
[1. Farmers' markets—Fiction. 2. Hispanic Americans—Fiction.] I. Gallagher-Cole,
Mernie, ill. II. Title.
PZ7.K678324Marc 2009
[E]—dc22
                                        2008030882

Printed in the United States of America in North Mankato, Minnesota.

092018   000939

Max
Goes to the
Farmers' Market

by Adria F. Klein
illustrated by Mernie Gallagher-Cole

Special thanks to our reading adviser:

Susan Kesselring, M.A., Literacy Educator
Rosemount–Apple Valley–Eagan (Minnesota) School District

PICTURE WINDOW BOOKS
Minneapolis, Minnesota

Max and his mom are at the farmers' market.

4

The market is filled with eggs, fruits, vegetables, and flowers.

Yellow

Purple

Oranges

Peppers

Beans

Potatoes

Max and his mom like to shop
at the farmers' market.

Local farmers grow the food and the flowers. They bring the food and flowers to sell.

Max and his mom look at all of the vegetables.

Mom picks some green lettuce.

Max and his mom look
at the carrots.

Mom picks a bunch of orange carrots.

Max and his mom look at the eggs.

12

Mom picks one carton
of brown eggs.

Max and his mom look
at all of the fruit.

Mom picks three red apples.

Max and his mom look
at the peaches.

Mom picks four orange peaches.

Max sees lots of flowers.

19

Max picks a pink flower for Mom.

The farmers' market is a
great place to shop!

23